Jack and the Wonder Beans

Jack and the Wonder Beans

written by James Still

drawings by Margot Tomes

G.P. Putnam's Sons · New York

Text copyright ©1977 by James Still
Illustrations copyright © 1977 by Margot Tomes
All rights reserved. Published simultaneously in
Canada by Longman Canada Limited, Toronto.
Printed in the United States of America

Library of Congress Cataloging in Publication Data
Still, James   Jack and the wonder beans
[1. Fairy tales. 2. Folklore] I. Tomes, Margot. II. Title
PZ8.S65Jac   [398.2]   [E]   77-7982
ISBN 0-399-20498-9

for
Teresa Lynn Perry,
Matthew Livings
and
Mark David Cadle

Way back yonder there was a widow woman and her son Jack and they were poor as Job's turkey. The way some tell it, their homeseat was here on Wolfpen Creek. Or around about.

Well, all Jack and his mam had was their home roof and a cow and a patch of land. They lived on garden sass and crumble-in made of plain bread and milk.

Now, hit come a rough winter. Cold as doorknobs. They had to eat the corn seed held out to plant the sass patch in the spring. And come spring, the cow went dry. Dry as a hat. Jack's mam said to Jack, "Take and sell the cow so we will have money for bread."

So Jack hung a sign betwixt the cow's horns: "Lady cow for sale anybody." He went up the road and down the road, through brush and saw-brier, aiming for to sell the critter. But dry cows are hard numbers to unload. And she was all hide and bones. A walking shikepoke.

Yet he had bids. Would he swap to a crippled hammer with one ear gone? No.

A poke for catching snipe? A gee-haw whimmy-diddle? Now, no. You can't eat airy a one of them.

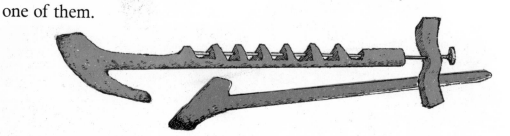

Then Jack got up with a gipsy who offered three beans for the cow. Not common beans. Not regular beans. "Wonder beans." So said the gipsy. "Sow them and they will feed you your life tee-total."

Now hit looked like Jack was being tooken. Ay, no.
Jack was no simpleton. As the saying goes, to get ahead
of Jack you would have to have long ears and a bushy
tail. Jack knew you couldn't buy wonder beans any day
of the week. And three beans beat nothing. Seeds for the
sass patch. So he swapped. Did Jack.

Here Jack comes home with no money and no cow.
No nothing except three beans. Fewer than fingers on a
hand. Did his mam throw a conniption! She sizzled like a
red-hot horseshoe in the cooling tub. And she took and
throwed the seeds out of the window. She hooted to Jack,

"Upon my word and deed and honor, you couldn't be trusted to pack slops to a sick bear! You don't know beans!" Jack quick jumped into bed and pulled the kivers over his head so as not to hear worse.

The next morning Jack he heered something rustling outside the window. He cracked his eyes. He saw something looked just like bean vines. Right! Right as a rabbit foot. They were bean vines. The beans had come up. They were twisted together into a stalk thick as a blacksmith's arm. The stalk reached above the window, above the eaves, the roof. Up and up it went. Up into the sky.

You know Jack. Independent as a hog on ice. Ready
for anything. He made to climb the beanstalk to see
where it went. Did Jack. Up and up. Up and up and up.
And directly he came to where the stalk leaned against a
path. And Jack he stepped onto the path and went where
it went. To a castle house. He went up the path and beat
on a big door. Hit was the biggest thickest door ever was.

Jack banged on the door and a woman opened it. A high tall giant woman. Of a size she could of put Jack in her apron pocket. Said Jack, cocky as they come, "Where's the master of this house place—your old man?"

And the high tall woman said, "He hain't come in yet, and woe when he does. He eats tadwhackers the likes of you. Boiled, fried, or baked in a pie. Any which way when he's hungry."

Now, Jack wasn't easily frightened, and he said, "Old Sister, I'm hungry myself. What's a-cooking?"

Well, what the giant woman done was feed him some crumble-in. Fed him three bowls. To fatten him. She would eat Jack herself. She'd make a stew. Seasoned with dill. And scarce had he finished than the biggest door ever was flew open and in walked a giant seventeen feet tall, with feet like cornsleds, hands like hams, fingernails to match bucket lids, and the meanest eye ever beheld in this earthly world.

The high tall woman quick popped Jack into the oven
to hide him. She'd not let her husband have a shred of
Jack. He would eat the meat and leave her the gristle.

The giant came in *tromp, tromp*. Sniffing and snuffing and snorting. He came a-saying:

> "*Fee, fie, chew tobacco,*
> *I smell the toes of a tadwhacker.*"

"You're smelling the crumbs in your beard from the two you wolfed down for breakfast," said the woman.

The giant said, "Humn." Even a giant knows when a
woman says something that's it. He set himself at the
table, and reached in under, and fetched out two flax
sacks of gold money. Emptied one on the table and began
to count. His wife she got busy polishing her kettle pot.
She was making her readys for a Jack stew. Sprinkled
with dill.

Counting beyond thirty-three will make any tom-body drowsy. Beyond ninety-nine hit's worse. By two hundred and twenty-two you're bedazed. Messing with figures always made the giant sleepy, and the more he counted the dozier he got. Pretty soon he was snoring. Jack caught his chance when the high tall woman stuck her head in the kettle to rub clean a spot. He jumped out of the oven. He grabbed a sack of gold and took off like Snider's hound. For the beanstalk. And nobody was in knowance of it.

Well, Jack and his mam bought a pretty cow with ribbons on her horns. They planted a sass patch. They lived in ease. They set on the porch and hung their feet over the banisters. That was the all they had to do. And I reckon you'd say they were satisfied tee-totally.

Not Jack. As the saying goes, he hadn't got his barrel full. And curiosity was stinging him. So one fine clever day Jack took his foot in his hand and gave it another crack. He clambered up the beanstalk. Up and up and up. Jack did.

When Jack knocked on the biggest thickest door ever there was the high tall woman. And her right proud to see him. He'd not sidestep her stew this time. Again Jack said, "Old Sister, I'm hungry, and what's cooking?" She

fed him five bowls of crumble-in. She'd fatten him plump. When the seventeen-foot giant showed up, she popped Jack into a skillet. A skillet the size to fry a whole beef. To hide him. And clapped on the cover.

The giant came in *tromp, tromp*. Sniffing and snuffing and snorting. He came a-saying:

> *"Fee, fie, pickle and cracker,*
> *I smell the toes of a tadwhacker."*

"You're smelling your upper lip," said the woman. "The grease from the couple you gobbled for breakfast."

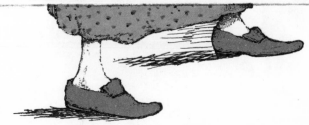

Even a giant with feet like cornsleds understands you can't out-argue a woman. So he hushed on that. He says, "Old wife, bring me my little banty hen that lays gold eggs." Even a woman big enough to tuck a boy in her apron pocket knows that when a man speaks he's spoken. So she brought the hen.

The giant says to the hen, says, "Hen, lay." The hen did. Laid a gold egg. And another and another every time he said to lay. The giant counted. And here he was messing with figures again. And he got sleepy.

The high tall woman she got out her kettle pot and
began to polish it for her Jack stew. Stew with dill. The
banty hen kept laying. The giant kept tallying. And fairly
soon the giant was nodding. And snoring. When the
woman had her head so deep in the kettle she couldn't
hear thunder, Jack caught his chance. He threw off the
skillet cover. The cover made a racket that would of
woke seven sleepers. The giant cracked his eyelids. And
Jack grabbed the little hen and lit out for the beanstalk.

The giant waked and took after him. And did Jack ske-daddle! You could of shot marbles on his shirttail.

Jack made it to the beanstalk with the giant shaving his heels. He came down the stalk in a shower of leaves and a hail of beans and the giant couldn't ketch up with him. When Jack tipped the ground he halloed to his mam, "Fetch the ax!" Jack's mam fetched a double-bitted ax which could cut coming and going.

Jack cut down the beanstalk with a single blow and
that was the end of the seventeen-foot giant with feet as
big as cornsleds and fingernails to match bucket lids and
the meanest eye in the world earthly.

And an odd thing! On earth the little hen would lay
only common brown eggs. Regular eggs.

Ay, no matter. Jack had his barrel full enough. And he
bought a second cow with ribbons to her horns. A pretty
cow. One to come fresh while the other was dry. They
lived on banty eggs and garden sass and crumble-in
thereinafter. And nobody could rightly say Jack didn't
know beans. Now, no.

DATE DUE			
Late			